THE KITTEN'S TALE

PET VET

Book #1 CRANKY PAWS
Book #2 THE MARE'S TALE
Book #3 MOTORBIKE BOB
Book #4 THE PYTHON PROBLEM
Book #5 THE KITTEN'S TALE
BOOK #6 THE PUP'S TALE

First American Edition 2010
Kane Miller, A Division of EDC Publishing

First Publishing by Scholastic Australia Pty Ltd in 2010
This edition published under license from Scholastic Australia Pty Limited
Text copyright © Sally and Darrel Odgers, 2010
Illustrations copyright © Janine Dawson, 2010
Cover copyright © Scholastic Australia, 2010
Cover design by Natalie Winter

For information contact:
Kane Miller, A Division of EDC Publishing
P.O. Box 470663
Tulsa, OK 74147-0663
www.kanemiller.com
www.edcpub.com
www.usbornebooksandmore.com

Library of Congress Control Number: 2010923987

Printed and bound in the United States of America
6 7 8 9 10 11 12 13 14 15
ISBN: 978-1-935279-76-1

THE KITTEN'S TALE

Darrel & Sally Odgers

Illustrated By Janine Dawson

Kane Miller
A DIVISION OF EDC PUBLISHING

Welcome to Pet Vet Clinic!

My name is Trump, and Pet Vet Clinic is where I live and work.

At Pet Vet, Dr. Jeanie looks after sick or hurt animals from the town of Cowfork as well as the animals that live at nearby farms and stables.

I live with Dr. Jeanie in Cowfork House, which is attached to the clinic. Smaller animals come to Pet

Vet for treatment. If they are very sick, or if they need operations, they stay for a day or more at the clinic.

In the mornings, Dr. Jeanie drives out on her rounds, visiting farm animals that are too big to be brought to the clinic. We see the smaller patients in the afternoons.

It's hard work, but we love it. Dr. Jeanie says that helping animals and their people is the best job in the world.

Staff at the Pet Vet Clinic

Dr. Jeanie: The vet who lives at Cowfork House and runs Pet Vet Clinic.

Trump: Me! Dr.  Jeanie's Animal Liaison Officer (A.L.O.), and a Jack Russell terrier.

Davie Raymond: The Saturday helper.

Other Important Characters

Dr. Max: Dr. Jeanie's grandfather. The retired owner of Pet Vet Clinic. He is away on holiday.

Major Higgins: The visiting cat. If he doesn't know something, he can soon find out.

Whiskey: Dr. Max's cockatoo. He is on holiday with Dr. Max.

Tom: A traveling salesman.

Patients

Magnus: A lost kitten.

Thumper Bluey: An escaped cat.

Map of Pet Vet Clinic

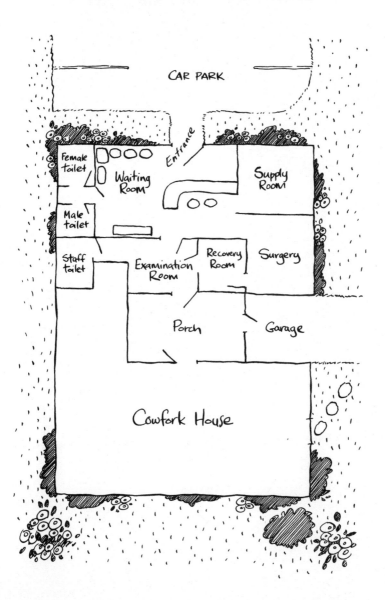

Chapter 1

Kitten on the Shelf

There was a kitten on the shelf in Pet Vet Clinic.

It all started when I went into the waiting room to snooze until Dr. Jeanie called me for morning rounds.

As I lay down, I sniffed the air. Higgins was here already! Usually he didn't arrive until after the first train pulled in at Cowfork station.

"Come out, Higgins!" I said.

"At ease, Trump!" said Higgins. He peered down from the shelf where

Dr. Jeanie stores old files. I could just see his ears and whiskers.

"Come down!" I bounced at the wall, pawing at the lower shelves.

"Stop that foolish bouncing," said Higgins.

"I am a healthy, young terrier," I explained. "Healthy terriers are meant to bounce." I bounced again.

There was a scrabbling sound on the shelf and a startled mew. Pieces of paper fell off.

"Is someone with you?" I asked. I detected a strange scent above me. "Who is it?"

"No one," said a voice. It sounded young.

"You have to be someone," I said.

"Stand clear, Trump," said

Higgins. He jumped down from the shelf, landing on his feet. Most cats can do that if they have time to prepare their jumps.

Higgins gave himself a few licks, then looked back to the shelf. "With me, Private," he ordered.

Nothing happened.

"Private!" said Higgins. "I gave you an order!"

A kitten's face popped into view over the edge of the shelf. "I can't, Major Higgins," said the kitten. "There's a *dog* down there. You know I'm afraid of scary dogs."

"This is Trump," said Higgins. "She's not scary. She's Dr. Jeanie's A.L.O."

"She bounced," said the kitten.

I sat down in good-dog position, with my front paws together. "I won't bounce at you if you come down," I said. "I only bounce at Higgins because we're friends. We call it the Enemies Game."

The kitten swiveled so his long tail stuck out over the shelf. He was about to jump when a sheet of paper slipped underneath him. He squawked as his hind paws skidded off the shelf, leaving him hanging by his front ones.

"Help!" he wailed, kicking the air.

"Drop!" ordered Higgins, but the kitten wouldn't. Papers slithered and floated around us as the kitten went on wailing.

Part of being an A.L.O. is knowing when a problem needs a human to solve it. But before I could bark for Dr. Jeanie, the waiting room bell jangled. A lanky man came in from the street. "Hello?" he called.

I didn't know him, but he looked helpful. I ran up to him.

The man laughed. He was a bit older than Dr. Jeanie, and he wore glasses and carried a small case.

"Hello, Trump!" he said. "I've heard about you from Beetle, but–"

The kitten squawked as it tried to scrabble back onto the shelf. The man looked up. "Looks like you need help," he said.

He put down his case, set a chair by the shelf and climbed so he could reach the kitten. "I've got you," he said. The kitten spat and scrabbled, but our visitor peeled it free just as Dr. Jeanie came in.

"What's all the commotion?" she asked. "Is that your kitten?"

The man grinned and stepped down from the chair. "It's not mine. I just rescued it from that shelf. I thought it was one of your patients."

Dr. Jeanie came to take the kitten.

"I've never seen him before," she said, turning it to face her.

The kitten spat at her.

I looked around for Higgins, but he had disappeared.

The man laughed. "Bold little thing, isn't he?"

"Yes." Dr. Jeanie turned the kitten again. "He's dirty and **malnourished**, though."

She looked hard at the stranger. "Are you sure you don't know anything about this kitten?"

Malnourished (mal-NURR-ish'd) —Animals or humans who don't get enough good food can become malnourished. This makes them thin and unhealthy.

"Not a thing," said the man. "I came in and saw this fellow claw-hanging from the shelf up there."

Dr. Jeanie examined the kitten. "No collar," she said. "I'd better put him in a cage and wait for his owner to claim him. That's if he has one."

"Do you think he hasn't?" asked the man.

"He might be a stray," said Dr. Jeanie, "although he doesn't seem particularly scared. More cross, I'd say."

The kitten spat again.

Dr. Jeanie and the man laughed.

"Anyway ..." said Dr. Jeanie. "If you haven't brought me a patient, what can I do for you? I have to go on rounds in a minute."

The man picked up his case. "I'm Tom Ashton—the new salesman for Petstuff Products."

"So, you took over from dear ol' Beetle?" Dr. Jeanie put the kitten in a spare climbing cage with a bed, a bowl of water and some kitty kibble. She fastened the door. "Come through to the office," she said, and led Tom out of the waiting room.

The kitten growled and glared at me. "*Now* look what you've done!" it spat.

Trump's Diagnosis. When cats jump or fall, they usually land on their feet. This is because they have a flexible spine and legs, and a special organ called a vestibular apparatus (vest-ib-you-lar app-a-rah-tis) in their ear. This works like the spirit level Dr. Jeanie uses to check if things are level. It tells the cat which direction to turn. But if a cat falls unexpectedly, it can't always land on its feet. It can be badly hurt, like a human or a dog.

Chapter 2

Magnus Is a Good Name

"We have a situation," said Higgins, slipping out of the toy box where he had hidden when Tom arrived. "My private is in prison. I blame you, Trump. You should have staged a diversion."

The kitten squalled crossly and clawed at the bars of the cage.

"That's not prison," I said. "It's a cage, with a bed and food and water." I turned to the kitten. "It's all right," I said. "You're safe. Just make yourself comfortable, and Dr.

Jeanie will—" I broke off. I had started the speech I make to our patients when they're nervous, but this kitten wasn't our patient. "What's your name?" I asked.

The kitten stopped clawing and curled his long tail around his paws. He looked sulky. "They call me Puss," he said. "I hate it."

"They?" I looked at Higgins. "What does he mean?"

"His people didn't give him a name," said Higgins. "I don't see them much, and they don't seem to want him. I just look out for him a bit."

"Major Higgins helps me find food," said Puss, "and he used to let me share his shed before his—"

"That's classified information,

Private." Higgins looked embarrassed.
He likes his tough-tom image.

"Yes, Major Higgins. Sorry, Major
Higgins," said the kitten.

Now that he'd stopped spitting
and clawing, I saw that he was about
half-grown, with fluffy fur and a long
tail and whiskers. As Dr. Jeanie said,
he was thin and bony.

He glared at me and lifted his front
paw, with the claws **unsheathed**.
"Stop staring, dog."

"I can't get you out of the cage," I said. "Dr. Jeanie will let you out when she finds your owners."

"I don't want her to

> **Unsheathed–**
> Unlike dogs, cats' claws are usually set in protective sheaths. They can push their claws out when they need to use them.

find them," said the kitten. "They shut me out at night, and a *dog* came." He shuddered. "It had big teeth, and it **treed** me. I was stuck up in the tree all night. Major Higgins saved me."

"That's why I brought the private here," said Higgins. "I wanted him to see that not all dogs are horrible to cats."

"But you said we might be able to

stay–" began the kitten.

Higgins glared at him. "That's confidential, Private."

"Of course we're not all

> **Treed**–When dogs chase animals like cats and possums, the animals often rush up trees to escape. The dogs sit underneath the tree and bark.

horrible to cats," I said. "But you cats could help yourselves if you stopped giving us feral looks and then running off. That makes us want to chase you. It's like the way *you* react, if a spider scuttles past your paws."

"Don't try chasing *us*, Trump," growled Higgins. "I already told the private it's not good to turn your back on an enemy. That's a sign of cowardice. The battle scars on a brave cat will always be on the nose and ears." He flicked his tattered ears.

I sat down in good-dog position again. "Does Puss live near you?" I asked Higgins.

Higgins shot the kitten a grumpy look and twitched his tail. "Maybe," he said. "But that's not the point. The point is, I brought him here to prove that not all dogs hurt cats, and you let Dr. Jeanie shut him up in a cage. What are you going to do about it?"

"I can't let him out," I said. "These cages are paw-proof and jaw-proof. Whiskey could undo it with his beak, but he and Dr. Max have gone on holiday. We'll have to wait for Dr. Jeanie."

Before Higgins could answer, Dr.

Jeanie returned to the waiting room with Tom.

"I'll be back through Cowfork next Wednesday," said Tom. He came over to the cage and poked his fingers through the bars.

"Careful," said Dr. Jeanie. "Scared kittens often bite." But Puss didn't bite Tom. He bumped his nose on Tom's fingers.

"I wonder if this fellow will still be here when I come back?" said Tom.

"I doubt it." Dr. Jeanie glanced at the clock, and I knew she was thinking about rounds. "If his owners don't come today, I'll try to find them."

"Well, I hope it all works out for him," said Tom. He wiggled his fingers. "I like this fellow. If he was mine, I'd call him ..." Tom closed his eyes and went off into a kind of daydream. "I'd call him Magnus. Magnus is a good name." He wiggled his fingers at the kitten again. "Hello, Magnus."

The kitten rubbed his whiskers against Tom's fingers. "I like him," he said to me. "He wouldn't let a horrible dog tree me."

"Well, Magnus, good luck!" said Tom. He shook hands with Dr. Jeanie, patted me, and went out.

Dr. Jeanie sighed. "Yes, good luck, Magnus!" she said. She picked up her notes from the counter and snapped her fingers to me. "Rounds," she said. "Coming, Trump?"

I whined gently. Of course I wanted to do rounds with Dr. Jeanie. But I wondered if I should stay at Pet Vet and keep the kitten company. I could give him advice on dealing with dogs. But the kitten would still be there after rounds. My mind was still chasing options when the telephone rang.

"Bother," said Dr. Jeanie, and she glanced at the clock again. "If Tom hadn't held us up, we'd be gone by now." She picked up the phone. "Pet Vet Clinic. Jeanie Cowfork speaking. Oh, hello, Mrs. Gibbons."

The person on the other end of the phone talked for a while, and Dr. Jeanie said things like, "I see, Mrs. Gibbons," and "That's not so good." I could tell she wasn't pleased. She pulled a pad and pen over to the phone and took notes. "Thumper Bluey. Is he one of your blue Burmese?"

Mrs. Gibbons talked more, and Dr. Jeanie looked worried. "A Marmaladus Rex. That's a Territorial King Cat, right?" she said. "You don't want the ranger involved since Thumper has been loose before? I'll tell you what I can do. I'll lend you a **humane trap**. No, not right now. I'm on my way out."

> **Humane trap** (HEW-mane trap)—A trap that catches a cat, or other animal, without harming it.

There was more talking on the phone. Dr. Jeanie looked crosser than ever. "I have to go. I have patients to see. But if you wait until lunchtime, you can pick it up then. All right. Goodbye."

Dr. Jeanie put down the phone

and held both hands up in the air. "Some people think they deserve special service!" she said to me. She went to get the humane trap.

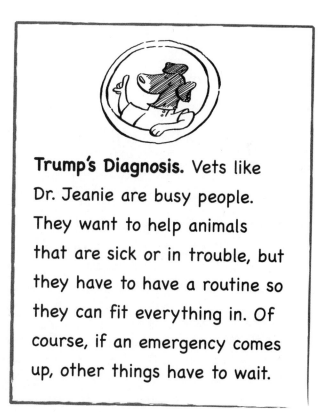

Trump's Diagnosis. Vets like Dr. Jeanie are busy people. They want to help animals that are sick or in trouble, but they have to have a routine so they can fit everything in. Of course, if an emergency comes up, other things have to wait.

ChaPter 3

Fang

Higgins came out as soon as Dr. Jeanie had gone.

"Why do you keep hiding?" I asked. "Dr. Jeanie won't hurt you."

"I lurk to listen and learn, Trump," said Higgins. "For example, I now have the intelligence that a Territorial King Cat is in the area."

"Why are you afraid of another cat?" I asked. "You're a brave and skilled warrior."

"I am," said Higgins, with a glance

at Magnus. "But part of a great warrior's strategy is to avoid trouble when possible. And mark my words, Trump, a Territorial King Cat is *trouble*. Some cats attack from fear or uncertainty. That's like **fear biting** in dogs. The Territorial King Cat is different. It is

> **Fear biting**–Some dogs bite if they think they are being threatened. This is called "fear biting."

afraid of almost nothing and almost nobody. Its one ambition is to conquer territory by fighting other cats. A King Cat leaves its victims frightened and bleeding."

I didn't like the sound of that. Neither did Magnus. He mewed with terror.

"Don't worry," I said quickly. "No cat can hurt you while you're at Pet Vet."

"Coming, Trump?" called Dr. Jeanie from the door.

I jumped up. Higgins could keep Magnus company until I came back.

Dr. Jeanie let me in to the front of the Pet Vet van. She put on my **safety harness**. Then we set off for our first visit.

Safety harness–If dogs travel in a vehicle, they should wear a safety harness. This is like a human seatbelt, but is designed for dogs.

Mostly, Dr. Jeanie and I visit farms and other places around Cowfork and Jeandabah, but today we had a call from outside Cookieton. The road ran beside the railway line, and Dr. Jeanie turned off past the station. "It might have been quicker to come by train," she told me. "We're looking for a place called *Gearings* in Clutterby Lane. Ah, there it is." I wagged my tail. I like it when Dr. Jeanie talks to me during rounds.

The lane was rough, and the van bounced as it hit potholes. Soon we reached what Dr. Jeanie calls a "smallholding," which is a very small farm. I usually like smallholdings. Owners with just a few animals can give them lots of individual attention. On the other hand, some owners find the animals take more time and work than they expected.

The owner of *Gearings* turned out

to be the second kind. He didn't look like a farmer, or behave like one. Dr. Jeanie undid my harness, and I jumped out of the van. I sniffed Mr. Gearings's shiny shoes, and he pushed me away. "It's about time," he said to Dr. Jeanie. "I expected you at nine."

Dr. Jeanie sighed. "Sorry. You have some steers that aren't well?"

"They're in the paddock," said Mr. Gearings. "They're skinny, and they cough a lot. How can I sell them like that?"

"You can't," said Dr. Jeanie. "Let's go and look."

I was about to follow them when I heard a growl, and a large dog raced up. It had its hackles up. "This is my place," it snarled.

Most farms have border collies or kelpies, but this was what my dad calls a bonehead, an angry dog with more teeth than brains. "I'm Dr. Jeanie's A.L.O." I explained politely. "I'm not trespassing. I'm here on business."

"I don't care what you are. Get off my patch." The bonehead snarled again and stalked forward with its tail stuck straight up and its fangs showing.

This was not good. Some big dogs hate smaller dogs. I wanted to run after Dr. Jeanie, but if I turned around, the bonehead might attack. I backed away. The bonehead slunk closer. I don't know what would have happened if Dr. Jeanie hadn't come back to the van for some medicine.

"Mr. Gearings, please call your dog off," she said sharply. "Sit, Trump."

I sat. The bonehead sneered at me.

"Mr. Gearings!" said Dr. Jeanie again.

Gearings whistled. "Fang! Come here, or I'll belt you."

The bonehead gave me a last glare and slunk over to his master. Gearings laughed. "Must have thought your dog was a cat. Fang hates cats, don't you, old sport! He's always chasing them. I got him as a watch dog."

Dr. Jeanie put me in the van. Then she went to the sick steers. "Those steers have lungworm," she said crossly to me, when she came back. "All of them. And Mr. Gearings says he can't spare the time to **drench** them until Saturday. And then he wanted to know if I had anything cheaper!" She shook her head. "Some people shouldn't have animals." She fastened my harness. "If I get another call out here, I'll leave you in the van, Trump. Dogs like Fang are trouble. Mr.

> **Drench**–To give medicine by mouth, by loading it into a drenching gun. Drenching guns look like water pistols, but hold medicine.

Gearings told me he chased a kitten up a tree last night. A *kitten*!"

I whined in agreement. Then I remembered Higgins had said the same thing about Territorial King Cats. And *then* I wondered if Fang was the dog that had treed Magnus. If he was, I didn't blame the kitten for being scared.

After rounds, we came back to Pet Vet. A smartly-dressed woman with high heels was waiting for us.

"You told me to come at twelve," said the woman.

"I said lunchtime," said Dr. Jeanie. "But I'll give you the trap now." She fetched the trap. "You see, it's mesh with a trap door. You put the bait in the front at first, but in the far end when you're ready to spring the trap."

"It will be ready right away, won't it?"

"Usually you put a trap out baited, but unset, for a few days first," said Dr. Jeanie. "That's so the cat feels confident about walking right in."

Mrs. Gibbons frowned. "Will you deal with it? I have other cats to look after. Silver Frost is about to have her litter, and my husband is away. I don't have time to spend days trying to catch Thumper."

"I don't either. You can call Jim Wolf if you prefer," said Dr. Jeanie. "He'll take care of it, for a price."

"No, no ... I'll do it." Mrs. Gibbons didn't pick up the trap, so Dr. Jeanie put it into the back of her fancy car. "Where should I set it?" asked Mrs. Gibbons.

"Wherever the cat has been seen. Ask permission before you put it on private property." Dr. Jeanie waved Mrs. Gibbons off, then came back to me. "Unbelievable!" she said.

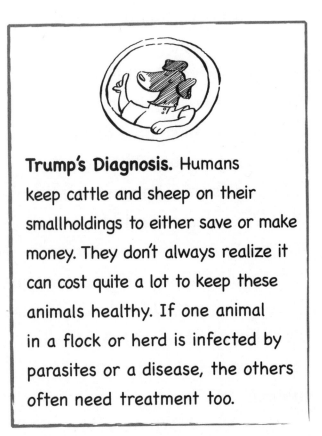

Trump's Diagnosis. Humans keep cattle and sheep on their smallholdings to either save or make money. They don't always realize it can cost quite a lot to keep these animals healthy. If one animal in a flock or herd is infected by parasites or a disease, the others often need treatment too.

CHAPTER 4

A CHECKUP FOR MAGNUS

Higgins was still in the waiting room when we opened the door for the clinic that afternoon, but he disappeared before the first patients came in. Magnus was curled up in his cage, purring slightly.

"Higgins?" I said, but there was no answer. I couldn't smell him either. I supposed he'd gone home. I didn't know exactly where Higgins lived. Whenever I asked, he said it was classified information. I thought

I might ask Magnus when he woke up. If it was near Clutterby Lane, then Fang probably was the dog who had treed him. I should warn Higgins to stay away from him. For now though, I had my duties as an A.L.O., so I followed the first patient into the **examination room**.

Examination room–The room where a vet examines and treats small animals.

The patient was a sheltie pup who had come for a checkup. Her breeders, Donna and Terri, were so calm and friendly I had nothing to do. Normally, I reassure pups that everything is all right and that Dr. Jeanie is there to help them, but this pup was happy. She wagged her tail at me, peeping out from under her long fringe of hair with bright eyes, then licked Dr. Jeanie's hand.

Dr. Jeanie was smiling as she handed the pup back to her owners. "She's fine," she said. "I'm sure her new owner will be delighted."

"Oh, she will," said Donna. "She's had two other pups from us over the years. We couldn't hope for a better home for Bluebell."

The ladies and Bluebell went out, and Dr. Jeanie came to rub my ears. "It's a funny thing, Trump, but whenever I start to think owners are either silly or neglectful, I am reminded that there are plenty who aren't."

After the last patient, I went to interview Magnus. He was awake, hanging by his front paws from the climbing frame in the cage. "I'm hungry," he said. He dropped to the floor and started crunching kitty kibble.

I was hungry too, but when I slipped outside to the back door where *my* bowl of kibble should have been, it was empty. I knew I hadn't finished it at breakfast, so I sniffed around for clues. It didn't take long to scent the thief. Higgins! Well! I thought. He only had to ask me if he was hungry. I supposed he'd stayed longer at Pet Vet than usual because of Magnus. I went back to see if Dr. Jeanie would give me more food and found her taking Magnus out of the cage. Did that mean his owners had come for him? I sniffed the air. Then I realized Dr. Jeanie was taking Magnus into the examination room. I followed.

"What's she doing?" Magnus asked, putting his ears back as Dr. Jeanie shone a small flashlight into his eyes.

"It's a checkup," I explained. "A pup came in for one this afternoon. It won't hurt. Dr. Jeanie will check your eyes, ears and teeth, and feel your tummy and legs. She'll see if you have fleas or mites and listen to your heart and lungs."

"Why?" asked Magnus, lifting one paw to scratch at Dr. Jeanie's wrist as she looked into his ear.

"Don't resist," I said. "This is a good

thing. Dr. Jeanie is making sure you are healthy. If she finds something wrong, she'll talk to your owners about it."

"They won't care. They shut me outside, and the scary dog treed me," said Magnus.

"Tell me about the scary dog," I said. "Was it a bonehead called Fang?"

"He didn't tell me his name," said Magnus. "He said he would eat me because I was on his patch. He had a lot of teeth."

"That sounds like Fang," I said. "Do you live near Clutterby Lane?"

"No," said Magnus. "I've decided I'm going to live with nice Tom and never get treed again."

"But you can't just decide things like that!" I said.

"I can," said Magnus. "Tom loves me. He gave me a name." He swished his tail. "The old owners didn't bother to do that. Someone gave me to them, and they didn't even want me. I *will* live with Tom."

I sighed. I didn't want Magnus to hope and then be disappointed. Then something occurred to me. Clutterby Lane was near Cookieton, not Cowfork or Jeandabah. "How did you get here?" I asked.

Magnus swished his tail again with annoyance as Dr. Jeanie felt his tummy. "I'm hungry," he said.

"But how did you get here?" I asked again.

"Major Higgins brought me after I got down from the tree," said Magnus.

I sighed. "Yes, but *how*? Did you walk? Because if you did, you can't have come from Cookieton."

"Oh, we came by—" Magnus broke off and narrowed his eyes at me. "That's classified information, Trump. Ask Major Higgins."

"I already have," I said. "He wouldn't tell me."

Magnus glared at me. "Then you shouldn't be asking me."

"Hmm," said Dr. Jeanie.

I pricked my ears. It sounded as if Dr. Jeanie wasn't happy with Magnus.

She looked at him and sighed. "I should wait for your owner, but I can't leave you like this," she muttered. "What do you think, Trump? Can we spare a bit of worm syrup and some flea and mite stuff?"

I whined and wagged my tail. If Magnus needed medicine, I thought Dr. Jeanie should give it to him.

"All right," said Dr. Jeanie. She opened the cupboard behind her and took out a bottle and spoon, a small syringe and a flannel bag with a drawstring. "In you go," she said, and popped Magnus into the bag with his head sticking out. He yowled and tried to claw at her.

"It's all right," I said. "Dr. Jeanie will make you feel better."

Dr. Jeanie tipped medicine into a plastic spoon and pulled gently on the scruff of Magnus's neck until he opened his mouth. Then she gave him the medicine. Magnus spluttered and spat. Next she used the syringe to drip oil into his ears. Finally, she took him to the tub in the hospital area, ran warm water, and dipped the bag, with Magnus still in it, into the tub.

Trump's Diagnosis. Like dogs, cats sometimes have parasites (**parr**-a-sites). These can be internal parasites like round worms and tapeworms, or external parasites like fleas and ticks. These parasites absorb food from the host. This can make the animal feel sick, or itchy, or hungry. Most animals get fleas or worms sometimes. Responsible owners treat their pets to control or kill the parasites.

Chapter 5

Gotcha!

After his bath and treatment, Dr. Jeanie put Magnus in the warming cupboard to rest while she disinfected the cage he had been in. When he was back in the cage, he gobbled a dish of cat food, lapped some water and then settled down to groom his fur.

He kept stopping to spit out bits of loose fluff. *Ptt! Ptt!* In between times, he'd glare at me.

"It's not my fault," I protested.

"Anyway, don't you feel better?"

"She *bathed* me," said Magnus.
"Cats are not meant to be bathed.
Major Higgins says so." He went
back to spitting out fluff.

I went to find Dr. Jeanie. She
was on the telephone. "He's about
fourteen weeks old," she was

saying. "Fluffy coat, long tail. No exotic breed … a nice little moggie. No one's been asking about him? Well, I'll keep him here for a few days. You can give our number to anyone who inquires, and I'll list him in the Lost and Found section of the paper." She hung up, then called the newspaper to describe Magnus all over again. Next, she took a photograph of the kitten and made a poster to stick up outside the clinic.

She read out loud as she wrote on the poster. "Found: one fluffy kitten, 12 to 14 weeks. Long tail."

I wished I could tell her not to bother. Magnus said if his owners came for him, he'd run away again.

I wanted to talk to Higgins about

him, but Higgins had gone. I supposed he was still angry with me. By bedtime, Magnus had stopped grooming and spitting. I went to see him while Dr. Jeanie checked the patients in the hospital cages and found him curled up in a basket. He was purring in his sleep.

I followed Dr. Jeanie through the door into Cowfork House, and we had dinner. I was hungry by then, since Higgins had eaten my kibble.

The next two days were busy, as usual. Two people who had lost cats came to inspect Magnus, but one said her cat was older, and the other said his cat had blue eyes. I half-expected Higgins to arrive very early on the first morning, but he didn't turn up until after his usual time, slipping through the window just as we left for rounds. I decided to talk to him as soon as we came home, but by then he'd gone. So had my kibble.

I was annoyed. Higgins has been coming and going mysteriously since I first came to Pet Vet with Dr. Jeanie. He acted as if he owned the place. He always tried to give me orders, but he hadn't stolen my food before. In fact, he'd claimed dog kibble was horrible because the pieces were too big. He must be taking it just to annoy me. I'd fix that!

On the second morning, I stayed behind when Dr. Jeanie left for rounds. I hated to miss out, but I had to confront Higgins. I hid while he slithered in through the window. I pricked up my ears while he had a word with Magnus. Then I went to stake out my bowl. Sure enough, Higgins sneaked around to the back door, pausing often to look over his shoulder. He behaved in exactly the way that makes terriers want to chase cats, but I am Dr. Jeanie's A.L.O., and A.L.O.s must behave with dignity when they're on duty. On the other hand, I wasn't on duty right then. I waited until Higgins reached my bowl. He darted a look from side to side. Then he crouched over my food and began to eat. I waited for him to get settled, then I sprang from my hiding place.

"Gotcha!" I yapped, and bounced at Higgins.

He gave a frightened yowl and leaped away, scattering kibble. His paws skittered on the path, and he wailed as he clawed his way up the nearest tree. I felt foolish. This wasn't supposed to happen. Higgins and I were old friends! He ordered me around, and I chased him out the window. He spat at me, and I yapped at him. That was the way it went. How had our bit of fun changed to stealing and real panic?

I sat down in good-dog position and whined. "Higgins? Come down!"

Higgins looked over his shoulder, spotted me, and relaxed. After a moment, he scrambled back down the tree and gave himself a few licks. "Missed it," he said.

"There's no need to panic," I said. "You know I won't hurt you."

Higgins looked at me blankly. "Don't be foolish, Trump. I wasn't running away from *you*. I was chasing a rat. It was—um—stealing your kibble. It escaped up the tree, and I chased it, but it got away. If you hadn't let out that silly yap, I would have had it."

I knew what I'd seen and what I'd smelled. There was no rat. *Higgins* had been stealing my kibble. *Higgins* had shot up the tree. But I pretended to believe him. I'd obviously startled him, and he didn't want to admit it.

He started grooming again, and I noticed he was less tidy than usual. He had a smudge down his white shirt, and he looked a bit thin and ragged around the edges. *How odd!* I thought. Was Higgins so worried about Magnus that he was neglecting his appearance?

"Besides," he said, between dabs of his tongue, "a warrior cat never turns tail on its enemy. That's why I had to face the rat."

"All right," I said. "I'll eat all the kibble so it doesn't attract rats."

"It won't come back," said Higgins.

"I don't suppose it will," I said. "But I'll eat it anyway." I settled to eat the rest of my food. "Want some?" I invited Higgins.

"No," said Higgins. "Dog kibble is horrible. It's quite unsuited to cats."

Trump's Diagnosis. Kibble is dry food that can be stored in a bag or a closed container. Cat kibble has smaller pieces and more fat in it because cats don't need quite the same diet as dogs. Kibble is good because it stays fresh for a long time if it is stored correctly. If you feed your dog or cat kibble, make sure it has plenty of fresh water available to drink.

Chapter 6

Caterwauling in the Night

Higgins didn't take any more of my food that day, so the next morning I did rounds with Dr. Jeanie. I didn't bother questioning Higgins on how Magnus had gotten from Clutterby Lane to Pet Vet. I knew he wouldn't tell me. Besides, maybe I'd gotten it wrong. Magnus had seemed to know Fang, but maybe he had just agreed to be polite.

After another two days, it felt as if the kitten had always been at Pet

Vet. Even Dr. Jeanie stopped asking our patients' owners if they knew where Magnus belonged. Some of the Thursday patients had wounds on their faces, so Dr. Jeanie began to warn the owners about the fierce cat. "I asked Katya Gibbons to let us know when she's caught him, but she might forget," she told her friend Cordelia Applebloom.

"I'll keep Dodger in the house," said Cordelia. "You know how he is. If there's an accident to happen, it will happen to Dodger." She pulled Dodger away from the climbing cage just before he stuck his nose through the mesh. It was just as well because Magnus had his fluffy hackles up.

Now that Dr. Jeanie had gotten

rid of his parasites, the kitten was putting on weight. He no longer cowered when a dog barked. He still hackled at strange dogs if they came close, but he greeted us each morning with a mew and a stretch and a friendly wave of his long tail.

On Friday, Dr. Jeanie checked Magnus over again and then let him out to play in the waiting room when it was quiet. I introduced him to my friend Dodger, who had come to the clinic with a stuffy nose. (He had broken a box of powder in Cordelia's bathroom.) I would have introduced him to a couple of other friendly dogs, but they had sore, bleeding noses, and they didn't want to be sociable. Magnus seemed

nervous of Dodger, but he didn't try
to hide in the shelves.

It was halfway through the
afternoon when I realized I hadn't
seen Higgins.

"Where's Higgins?" I asked
Magnus. "I haven't seen him for a
couple of days."

"The major had to make a sortie behind enemy lines," said Magnus. "He would have taken me if I hadn't been caged up in prison camp."

It took me a while to work this out. "What's Higgins after?" I asked.

"He's liberating supplies," said Magnus.

So that's why Higgins had stolen my kibble and then lied about it, I thought. He was playing his warrior-cat **game** with the kitten.

Game—Older cats sometimes play games with kittens to teach them how to act. Mother cats let their kittens pounce on their tails. This teaches the kittens about hunting.

"I suppose he'll come back and tell us how he stole a whole smoked salmon from Cordelia Applebloom's pantry," I said. Then I forgot about it because another patient came in. Dr. Jeanie put Magnus back in the cage, and I went back on duty.

When the last patient left, Dr. Jeanie cleaned up and wrote in her notes. She checked the hospital cages and said goodnight to Magnus. Then we went through to Cowfork House for our dinner.

I was dozing in my basket when I heard a distant shriek. My head snapped up, and I leapt to the door without even thinking about it. I couldn't get out, so I sat down to identify the noise. It might have been the squeal of car tires. Or maybe it was a startled bird. But it might be a Distress Call from an animal in trouble. In the seconds it took for me to think this, the sound came again, and this time the hackles stood up on my neck. Listening closely, I detected snarls and squawks and savage spitting. It came from Jeandabah Park, where Dr. Jeanie and I go to play Frisbee.

I rushed into Dr. Jeanie's bedroom and barked to wake her.

Dr. Jeanie yawned and rolled over. "Hush, Trump. It's the middle of the night."

I kept barking and ran back and forth to the outside door. Finally, Dr. Jeanie got up and pulled on a coat. She was a bit grumpy, but she followed me. "Sit," she told me, and opened the door.

Now even Dr. Jeanie could hear the **caterwauling** in the park.

"That sounds bad," she said. "Normally I'd ignore it, but with

> **Caterwauling** (Cat-er-walling)– Caterwauling is the horrible howling noise cats make when they are angry or agitated. Humans can't hear nearly as well as dogs.

that Marmaladus Rex around, I'd better check." She put on her boots, and we jumped into the Pet Vet van. Dr. Jeanie drove slowly, with the window down, so she could follow the noise. When we reached Jeandabah Park, she got out, clipped on my leash, and took one of her bags from the back of the van.

The caterwauling was close now. It was mixed with squawks and loud mews. I wanted to run ahead, but Dr. Jeanie wouldn't let me. "*No*, Trump. You could get hurt." She switched on her big flashlight, and we hurried into the park.

The humane trap jerked and shook in the flashlight beam. There was a strong smell of mackerel and an even stronger smell of tom cat. A huge shape was fighting and clawing inside the cage.

I stared. Was that orange striped creature really a *cat*? It was huge!

Dr. Jeanie seemed nervous too.
"Thumper Bluey, I presume?" she
said, raising her voice over the
squalling. "I should leave you here
for Katya Gibbons, but knowing
her, she mightn't come back until
lunchtime tomorrow, and by then ..."
She didn't finish the sentence, but I
could imagine the end. *By then you*

might have escaped. The thought of an angry Thumper Bluey clawing out of the cage and attacking us made my hair stand on end.

Dr. Jeanie put on thick gloves and reached for the cage. A pawful of huge claws shot out at her.

"Right. I'm not even going to try carrying you in this cage," she said. "A small, enclosed carrier seems better." She tied me to a bush, then went back to the van and fetched a cat carrier with a sliding door at one end and a clear window at the other. She clamped the open end to the door of the humane trap and then raised the trap's door. "In you go," she said, and hit the other end of the trap with a stick.

Suddenly, I remembered my duty. I didn't like Thumper Bluey, but he was a frightened animal, and I should try to calm him down. "It's all right, Thumper," I said. "Go into the carrier. Dr. Jeanie will get you home to Katya Gibbons."

Thumper Bluey shot into the carrier. I think he thought the clear window was an opening because he bounced off the end with a snarl. I found myself almost nose to nose with him. Although he was in a cage, I was as scared as I'd been when I encountered Fang. I wondered what would happen if Fang and Thumper met.

Thumper stared at me and hissed. He had something fluffy stuck in his teeth. "Victory!" he snarled. "I won the Battle of the Mackerel! I vanquished the foe!"

Dr. Jeanie slid the door down and locked it into place with a snap. Then she turned to the humane trap and tried to pick it up.

"Whoops!" she said, as one end swung to the ground. "Katya must have weighted this." She dropped the trap and something yowled and shot out the open end.

Still wailing, it vanished into the bushes.

"What was that?" asked Dr. Jeanie.

I stared after it. My nose told me it was Higgins.

Trump's Diagnosis. Animals have different personalities, but they can also have breed characteristics. Jack Russell terriers like me were bred to hunt. We bark and dig and investigate. Some kinds of dog were originally bred to fight, or to guard. Modern dogs want to do the same things. Knowing what an animal was bred for helps you understand its behavior.

ChapTer 7

FinDing Higgins

"Oops!" said Dr. Jeanie. She looked around, then shrugged.

Dr. Jeanie left me tied up while she carried Thumper and her bag to the van. She came back for the trap. I was worried. Higgins had been fast, but I knew he was hurt. I smelled blood. I whined and pulled at my leash, but I couldn't get loose.

"Higgins!" I called, but Higgins didn't answer.

I tried to slip away from Dr.

Jeanie when she came for me, but she had a firm grip. "No, Trump. We caught the monster, but I don't want you disappearing. Let's get back to bed." We drove back to Pet Vet.

Thumper ranted about victory and battles all the way.

"What did you do to Higgins?" I asked, but he just spat at me. I realized he had some of Higgins's fur caught between his teeth.

Dr. Jeanie locked Thumper in the storeroom. "I'm not having you terrorizing the other patients," she told him. She wrote a note for Davie, our Saturday helper, and stuck it to the door. "DO NOT OPEN THIS DOOR," she read aloud. Then we went to bed.

When Davie came the next morning, he was excited about Thumper. "I wish *I'd* been there," he kept saying, as he scrubbed hospital cages. "Can I feed him, Dr. Jeanie?"

"No," said Dr. Jeanie. "He's going home to Mrs. Gibbons. And this time I hope she *keeps* him there. Telephone her, Davie. Tell her to come and get her cat."

Davie did so, and I went to talk to Magnus. "Private Magnus!" I said. I tried to sound like Higgins.

"Don't be silly, Trump," said Magnus, yawning. "You're a dog. You can't be part of the **clowder**."

"This is serious," I said. "Higgins is

Clowder–A group of cats.

in terrible trouble. I have to know where he lives."

"That's classified," said Magnus.

"Magnus!" I bounced and yapped before I could stop myself. Magnus hissed.

"Sorry," I said. "But tell me. Major Higgins's life might depend on it. He was in the trap last night with Thumper, and I'm sure Thumper bit him."

"Major Higgins has scars already," said Magnus proudly.

"But this is a bite!" I said. "Cat bites can turn **septic**.

> **Septic** (SEP-tic)–
> Infected with bacteria.

If Higgins doesn't get treatment, he could die."

"Major Higgins knows that," said Magnus.

"That's what worries me," I said. "Why didn't he come to Dr. Jeanie right away, instead of running off? Why didn't he send me a Distress Call? If he was losing blood he might be hiding somewhere, but he's probably gone home."

Magnus looked worried.

"Come on, Magnus," I urged. "Tell me! Where does he live?"

"Nowhere!" blurted Magnus. "I mean, he says he used to live near me, but then the Colonel died, and the Colonel's lady went away. Higgins didn't want to go and so he stayed."

"What are you talking about?" I asked. "Was the Colonel a cat?"

"No, he was a human. Major Higgins has been camping out in the shed for a long time, but now that horrible dog has moved in next door …"

"Oh," I said. It had never occurred to me that Higgins might be homeless. "But how did you get here from Cookieton?" I asked.

Magnus scratched his ear and looked into space. "That's classified."

"This is a matter of life or death," I reminded him.

"We rode the iron horse," said Magnus.

"Oh, the *train*," I said. "So that's why Higgins used to come in after the first train!"

Magnus flickered his ear. "Don't tell Major Higgins I broke protocol," he said. "But since we left, he told me he's been lying low where the sneezy dog lives."

"Dodger's place!" I said. "I'll go around there right away. Don't worry. I won't tell Higgins you told me."

After that, Katya Gibbons arrived for Thumper Bluey. Davie helped her carry the cage to her car, and I nipped behind them and raced to Dodger's place. Dodger was shut in, so I talked to him under the door. "Dodger, do you know where Higgins is?"

Dodger sneezed. "Who's that? I can't smell you."

"It's me, Trump. I think Higgins is hiding out here. May I track him down?"

"Of course," said Dodger. He sneezed again. I thought of Fang and was glad I lived near Dodger instead.

Dodger is as big as Fang, but he has manners.

Having gotten Dodger's permission, I sniffed around his territory. I soon picked up Higgins's scent. He had come through the gate and gone to ground in Cordelia Applebloom's woodshed.

"Higgins?" I called. "It's me, Trump."

There was silence.

"Higgins, I know you're hurt. You have to see Dr. Jeanie."

There was more silence.

"Private Magnus is worried. What if his owners come for him and you're not there to advise him?"

Finally Higgins spoke. "Go away, Trump. Magnus is better off without me."

"He's not!" I said. "You saved him from the dog. You brought him to Pet

Vet so Dr. Jeanie could help him."

Higgins moaned. "Let me die in peace."

I didn't like the sound of that. "Attention, Major!" I said. "It's your duty to advise Private Magnus."

"Go away!" said Higgins. His voice sounded hoarse. "I'm dying, and I'm shamed. I'm not worth saving."

"Don't be silly," I said. "How can you be shamed? No one could beat Thumper Bluey in a fight. You were very brave to challenge him."

"I didn't," said Higgins. "I was hungry, all right? I went after the mackerel, and then that monster came in after me. He bit me on the rump! He would have killed me if he hadn't been so wild about being trapped.

Now do you see why I have to die? A rump wound is the mark of a coward."

"But you didn't turn to run," I said. "You were foraging and fell victim to a cowardly attack from the rear." I let him think about that for a bit, then added, "Come on, Higgins. We need you."

At last Higgins crawled out of the wood pile. He looked sick and

miserable, but he limped after me to Pet Vet.

Dr. Jeanie looked at me, and then at Higgins, and groaned. But she picked him up gently and took him into the examination room.

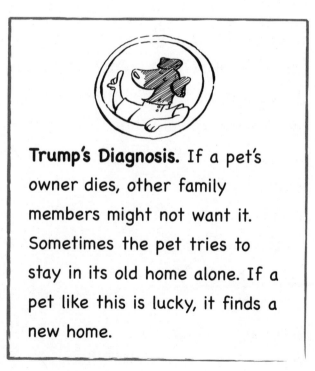

Trump's Diagnosis. If a pet's owner dies, other family members might not want it. Sometimes the pet tries to stay in its old home alone. If a pet like this is lucky, it finds a new home.

Chapter 8

Magnus Goes Home

Higgins was sick for a few days, but Dr. Jeanie gave him medicine to cure the infection. "I don't suppose *your* owners want you either," she said, stroking him. "You hang around here most of the time anyway, but it looks as if you've been living rough."

She put Higgins in a hospital cage next to Magnus.

On Wednesday, quite early, the bell jangled, and a man put his head around the door. "Dr. Jeanie?"

It was Tom the salesman, and I ran to greet him. Tom patted me, and then he saw Magnus in his cage and smiled. "You're still here, Magnus! I was hoping you would be."

Magnus started to purr loudly. "Tom's come!" he told me.

Dr. Jeanie came out. "Hello, Tom. Yes, no one's come for him yet."

"Well … can I take him, then?" asked Tom.

Dr. Jeanie stared at him.

"You see," said Tom, "I was thinking about him while I was on the road. I have room for a pet at my cottage, so why not?"

"I suppose it might work," said Dr. Jeanie. "He had a few problems, but they're fixed now. He needs

immunizations, but–"

Tom held up both hands. "It's okay. I

> **Immunizations**
> (IM-you-nize-a-sh'ns)–Medicine to prevent disease.

know about that. I had cats when I was young. Give him what he needs. I'll pay for his other treatment too." He turned to the door. "I brought a Petstuff pet carrier with me, in case."

"Just a minute," said Dr. Jeanie. "Tom, you spend several days a week away from home, don't you?"

"Yes, but I'm usually home on Wednesdays and Sundays. Why?" Tom raised his eyebrows, then nodded. "Oh, I see! That's why I would rather have a cat than a dog.

Cats are less dependent on human company. But Magnus will be well looked after. My friend Felicity comes to water my plants and practice the piano every day. She'd be happy to look after him. And I'll install a cat flap."

"That's fine, then," said Dr. Jeanie.

"And I'll get another cat so he'll have company," Tom went on. "I don't suppose you know of any nice cat that needs a home?"

Dr. Jeanie looked at Higgins. "Maybe I do," she said. "He's a bit battle scarred, but he has manners. I suspect he had a good home at some point, but he lost it somehow."

Tom came to stand by Higgins and held out his finger. "Hello, old soldier."

Higgins bumped his whisker cushion on Tom's finger. Then he began to purr.

Tom grinned at Dr. Jeanie. "Looks like I need another cat carrier and some kibble and bowls and things. I'll have to buy the kibble, and then we can all go home." He went out cheerfully.

Dr. Jeanie looked at me and smiled. "We're going to be late for rounds again, Trump, but in this case it's *really* worth it."

Actually, we were later still, because just then, Mr. Gearings came in with a sad and sorry bonehead. It looked as if Fang *had* met up with Thumper Bluey.

Authors' note

Most of the animal breeds in
the Pet Vet series do exist, but
as far as we know, there is no
such thing as a Territorial
King Cat.

About the Authors

Darrel and Sally Odgers live in Tasmania with their Jack Russell terriers, Tess, Trump, Pipwen, Jeanie and Preacher, who compete to take them for walks. They enjoy walks, because that's when they plan their stories. They toss ideas about and pick the best. They are also the authors of the popular Jack Russell: Dog Detective series.